ABOVE AND BELOW

―――――――― or ――――――――

Apocryphal Journeys in Thirty Etchings

Alexander Massouras

Above and Below

1. In Flight
2. A Trip Down
3. The Invisible Land

1

IN FLIGHT

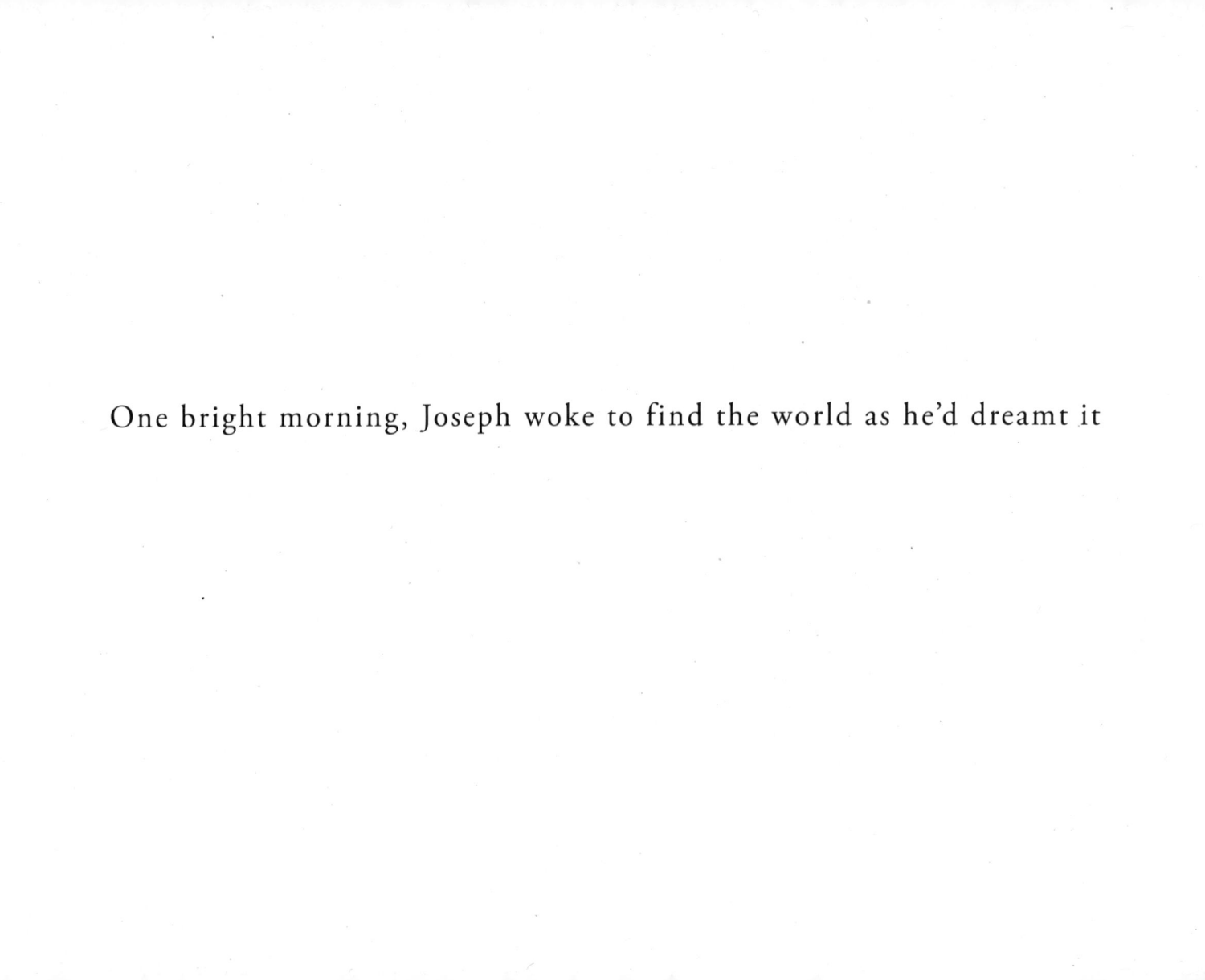

One bright morning, Joseph woke to find the world as he'd dreamt it

Fig. 1

(except for the passing knight).

Fig. 2

The familiarity soon grew oppressive,

Fig. 3

so Joseph discovered the secret of flight and flew away.

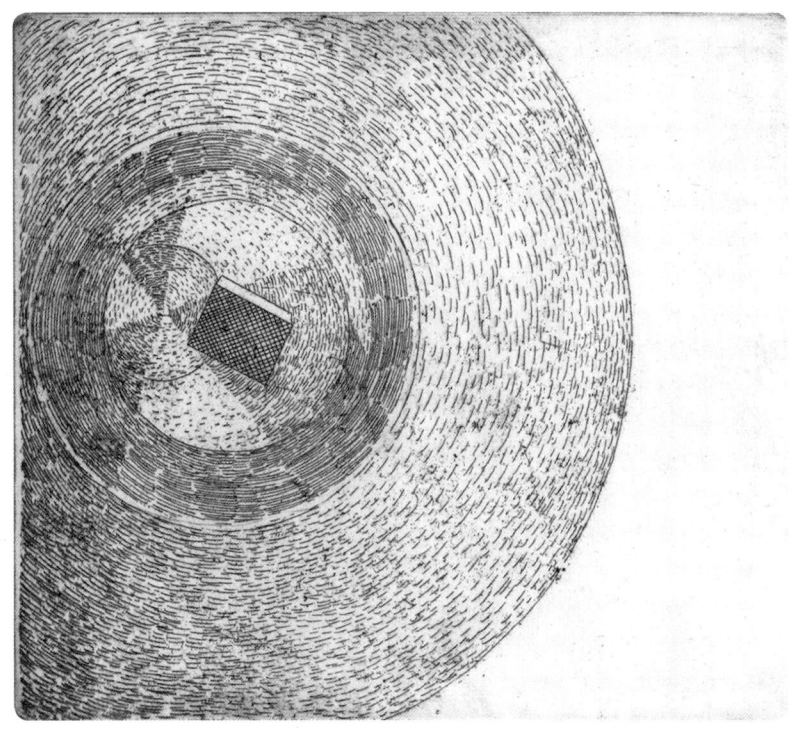

Fig. 4

High up in the clouds, it was silent. When the balloon moved with the breeze, the balloon felt still,

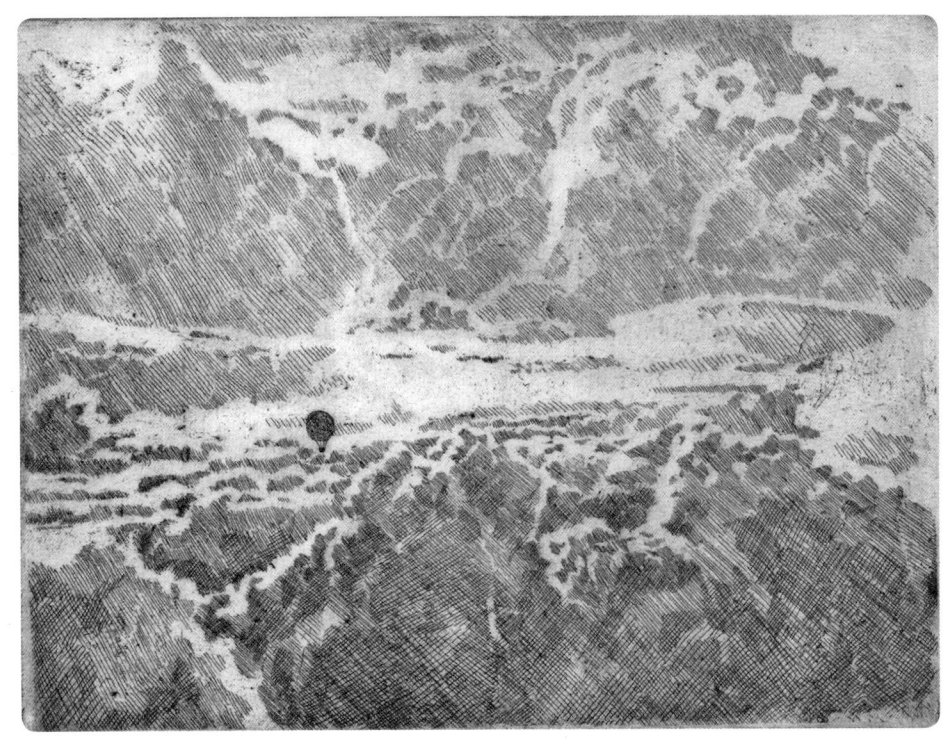

Fig. 5

and when there was no breeze, it was still.

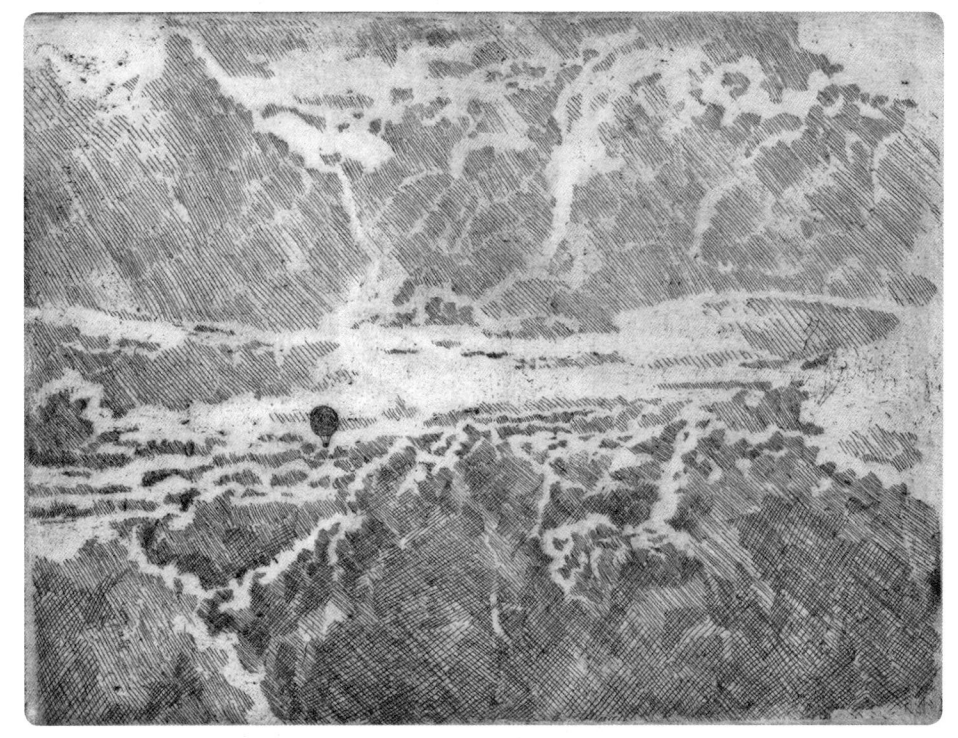

Fig. 6

The flight passed without event until a strange and ecstatic bird collided with the balloon, and both fell.

Fig. 7

It was winter. At dawn, Joseph found himself in an enchanting land,

Fig. 7

It was winter. At dawn, Joseph found himself in an enchanting land,

Fig. 7

It was winter. At dawn, Joseph found himself in an enchanting land,

Fig. 7

It was winter. At dawn, Joseph found himself in an enchanting land,

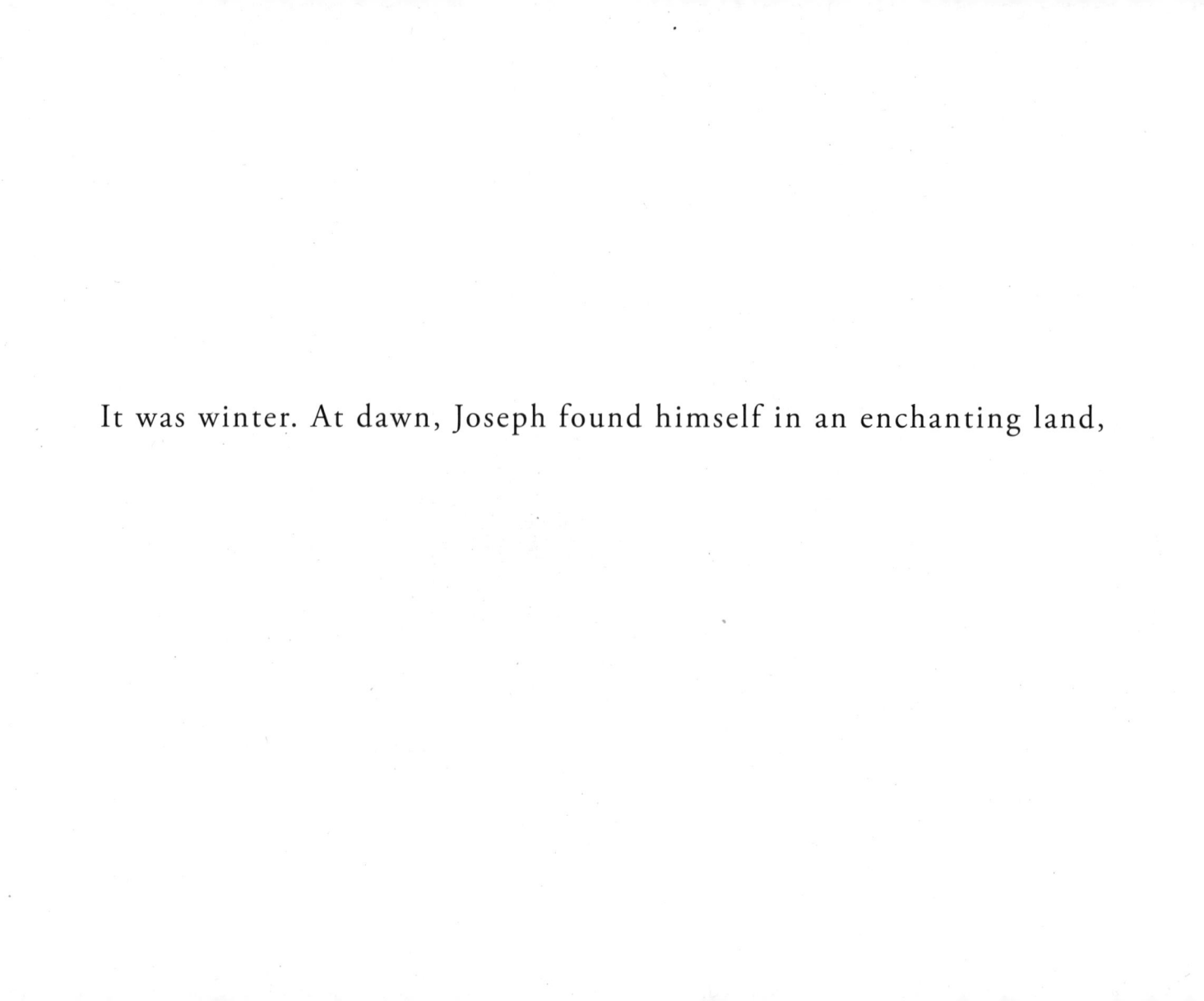

Fig. 8

which looked a lot like home.

Fig. 9

Fig. 9

2

A TRIP DOWN

'How do you describe a hole?' Evelyn wondered,

2

A TRIP DOWN

'How do you describe a hole?' Evelyn wondered,

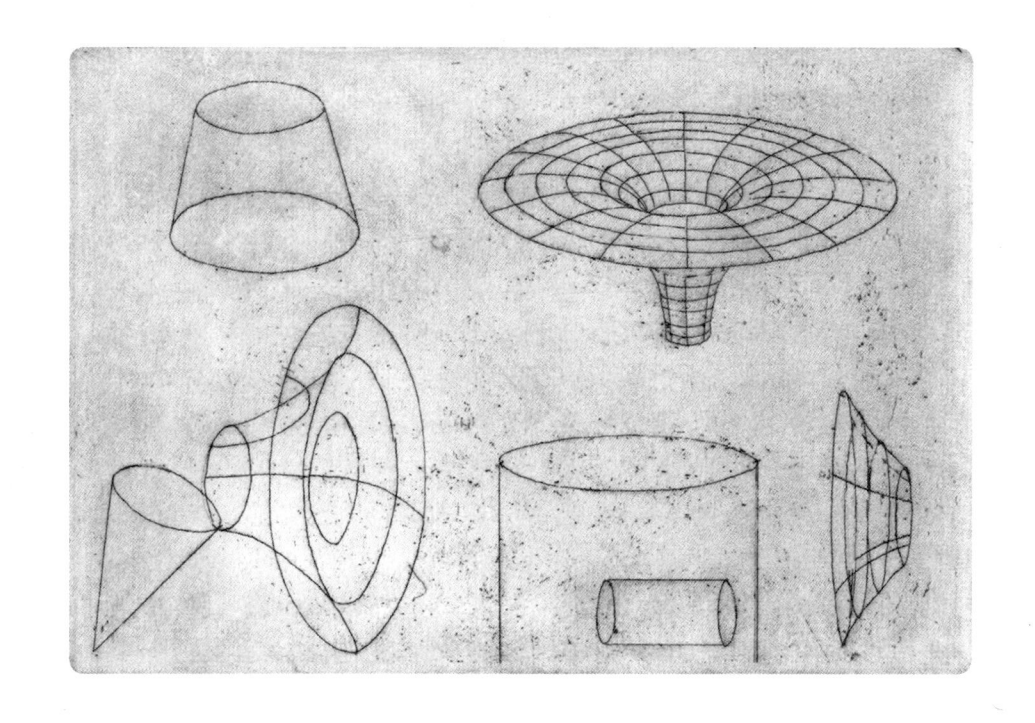

Fig. 10

before falling into one.

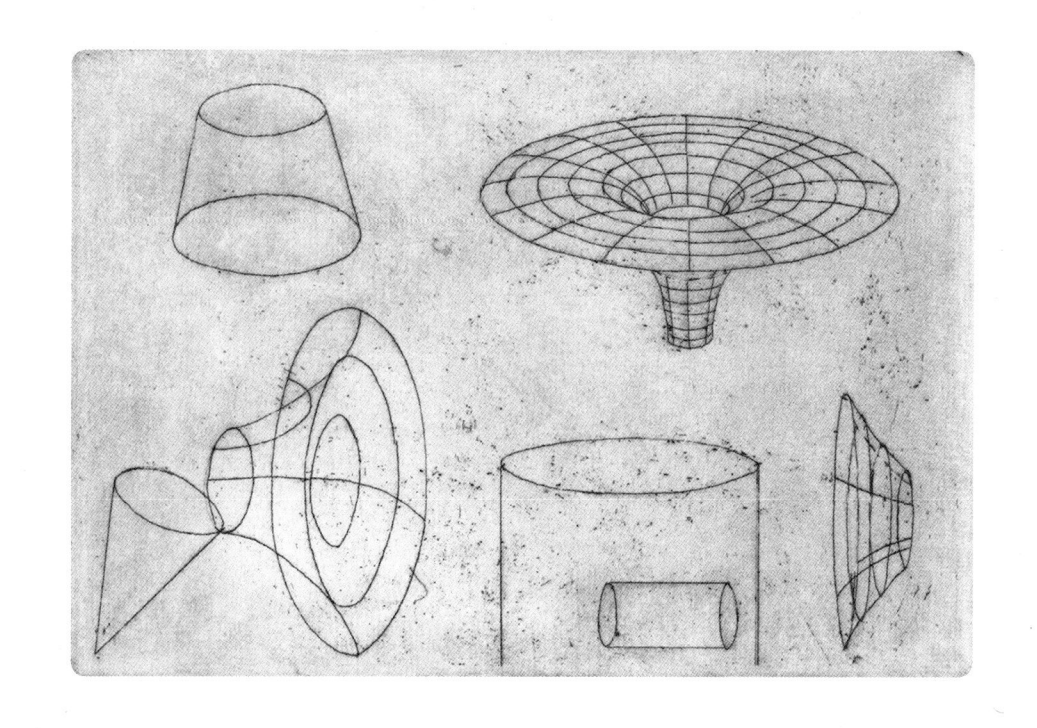

Fig. 10

before falling into one.

Fig. 11

'Is it possible to have a hole within a hole?' she thought.

Fig. 11

'Is it possible to have a hole within a hole?' she thought.

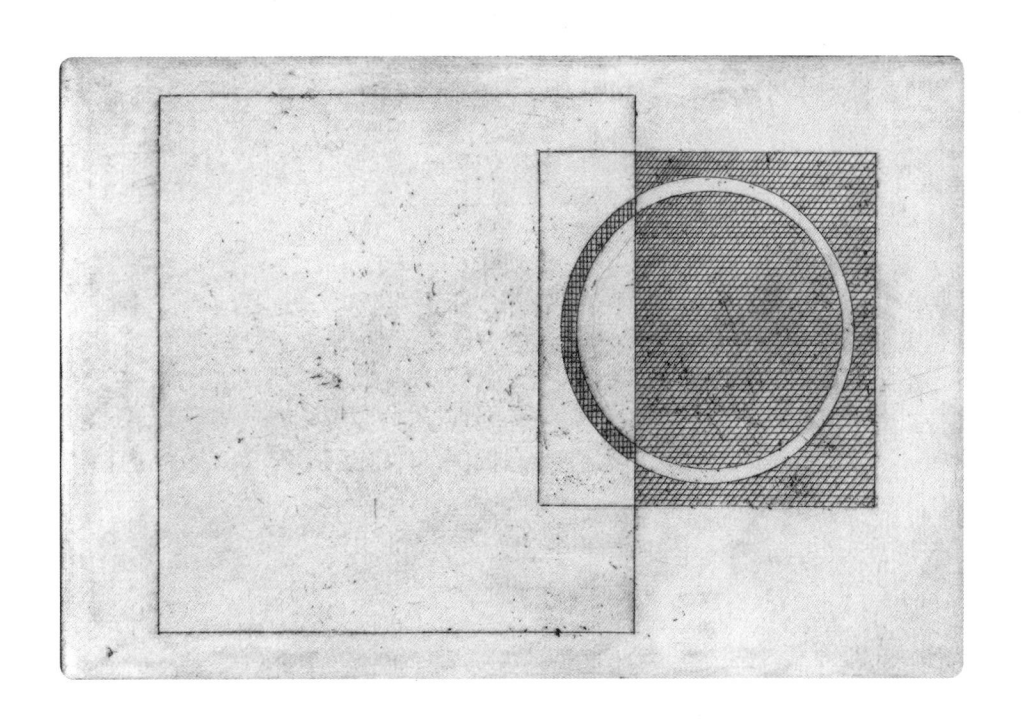

Fig. 12

And down she went again.

Fig. 13

In the darkness she could see clearly:

Fig. 13

In the darkness she could see clearly:

Fig. 13

In the darkness she could see clearly:

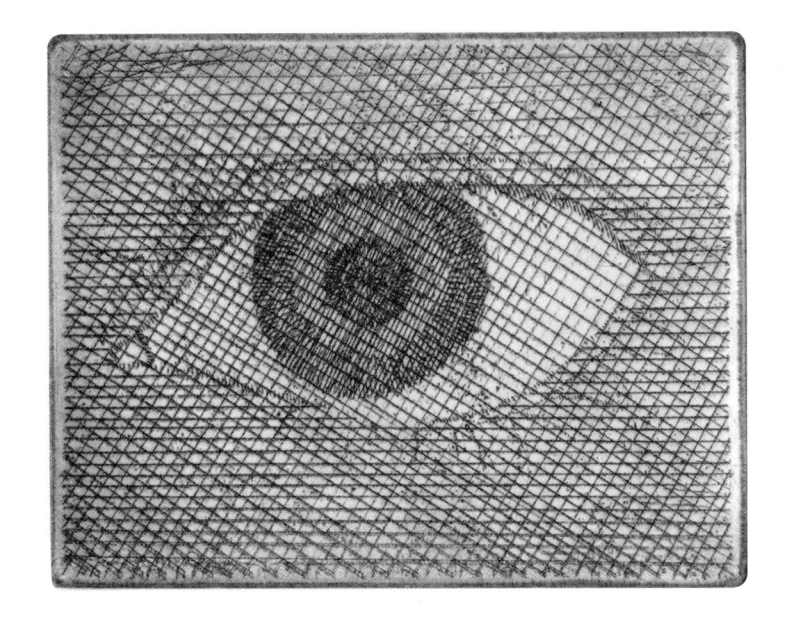

Fig. 14

'I am in a desolate hole, and I have been foolish', she said, as a bystander peered in.

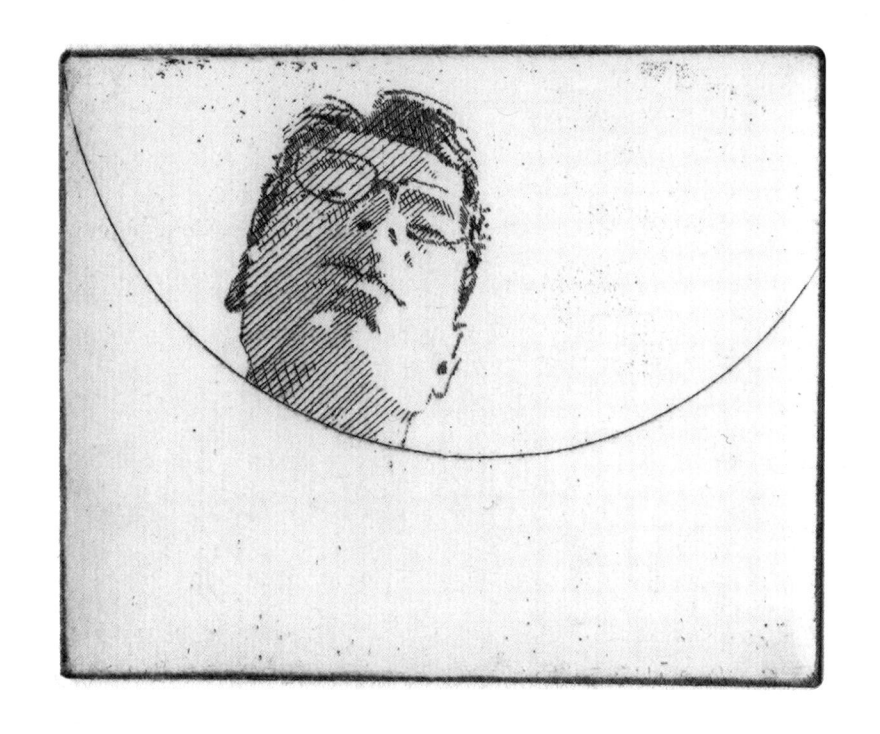

Fig. 15

'I have buried myself in worry and imagined problems into being'.

Passers-by shouted down and offered
their help, but Evelyn fell silent.

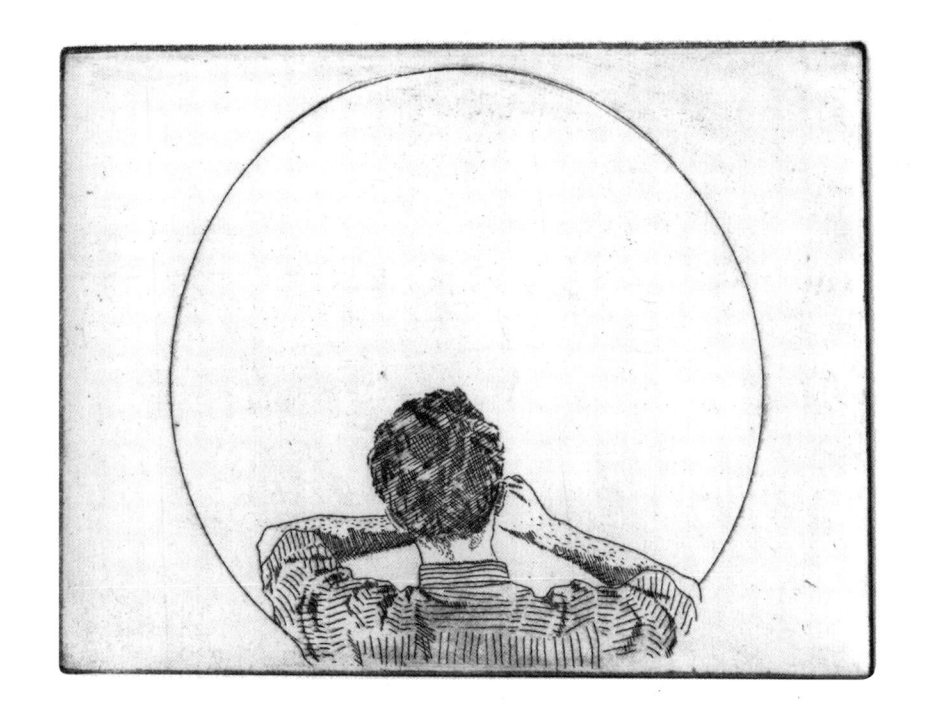

Fig. 16

Fig. 17

Evelyn thought of the things she used
to be and the places she used to go,

Fig. 18

and about why there were holes where no holes should be.

Fig. 19

Above, a glorious mechanism was devised to haul her out.

Fig. 20

Evelyn emerged from the hole, and all the joy and loveliness came back.

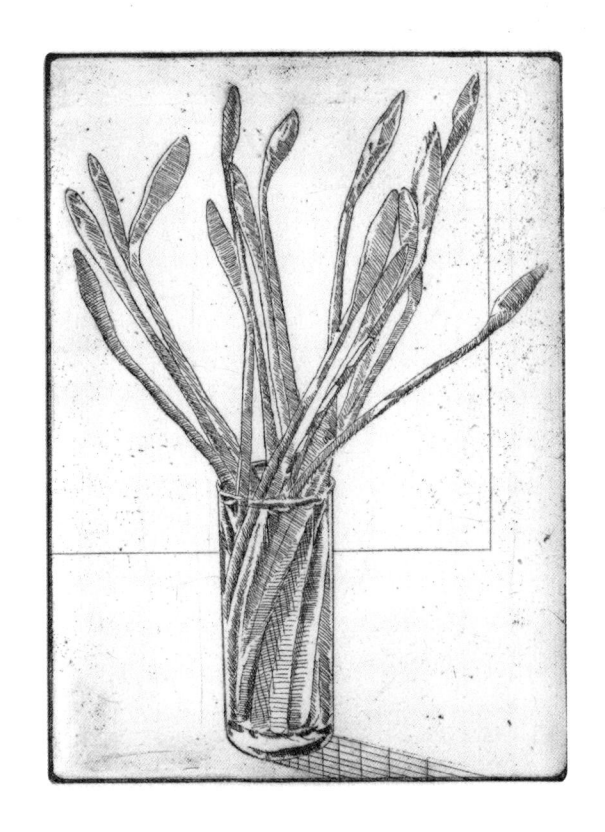

Fig. 21

3

THE INVISIBLE LAND

Televisions warned of rising tides.

Fig. 22

For a long time, Hans mistook these broadcasts for farce and ignored them.

Fig. 23

Then he started to notice the dead birds.

Fig. 24

It seemed that things weren't as they ought to be.

Fig. 25

Hans contemplated building a boat but lacked the timber.

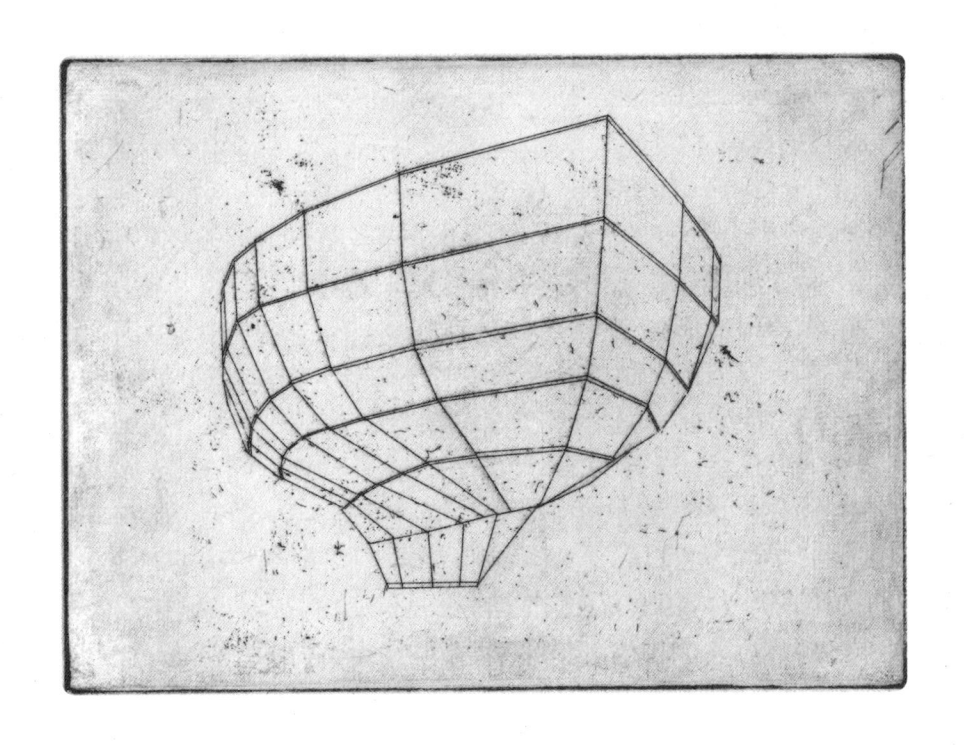

Fig. 26

So he covered up his pictures and set out for higher ground,

Fig. 27

above the invisible land.

Fig. 28

At what remained of the summit, he pitched his tent and settled,

Fig. 29

staying long after the floods receded and the landscape returned.

Fig. 30

Images: thirty hard-ground etchings
Edition of 60 plus 5 artist's proofs
Image size: 150 x 200 mm; 100 x 150 mm; and variants
Sheet size: 190 x 275 mm

First published in 2013 by Julian Page
www.julianpage.co.uk
Printed in England by Ex Why Zed on recycled paper
© Alexander Massouras and Julian Page 2013
All rights reserved

No part of this book may be reproduced or transmitted in any form or by any means, electronic or mechanical, including photocopying, recording or any other information storage or retrieval system, without prior permission in writing from the publisher.

A full catalogue record of this book is available from the British Library.
ISBN 978-0-9570124-1-7

JULIAN PAGE FINE ART